The Scent
of Your Breath

Melissa P.

Translated by Shaun Whiteside

D0813006

A complete catalogue record for this book can
be obtained from the British Library on request

The right of Melissa P. to be identified as the author of
this work has been asserted by her in accordance with the
Copyright, Designs and Patents Act 1988

Copyright © 2005 by Fazi Editore srl, Rome
Translation copyright © 2006 by Shaun Whiteside

Originally published in Italian by Fazi Editore in 2005
under the title *L'odore del tuo respiro*

First published in this English language edition in 2006 by
Serpent's Tail, 4 Blackstock Mews, London N4 2BT
website: www.serpentstail.com

Designed and typeset by Sue Lamble
Printed in Italy by ChromoLitho

ISBN 1 85242 916 X
ISBN 978 1 85242 916 4

10 9 8 7 6 5 4 3 2 1

To Thomas, who knows how to sniff my skirt,
to my mother the forest,
to my sister the storm,
to my Nonna Madonna.

So go, take the train
'cause if you don't go now, you surely will

Virginiana Miller, *Elsewhere*

I threw myself into the streets of the world with a bee in my hair. A bee that buzzed among my tresses, beat its wings convulsively and buzzed, buzzed, buzzed. And I didn't brush it away, I let it build its hive in my head, and everyone who met me said, 'You've got hair like honey,' and didn't know that there was a bee in my head, rolling round playfully among my thoughts with its soft, bi-coloured body. And it kept me company, my bee did, it became an indispensable if not very trustworthy companion: sometimes it gave me little bites on the back of my neck that should have hurt me. But my bee was too small to hurt me; it left honey in me, but never poison.

One day the bee whispered something in my ear, but it was too faint a murmur for me to hear. I never asked what it had tried to say to me, and now it's too late, my bee flew away from my hair, all of a sudden, and a passer-by killed it. It was squashed. And on the white marble I can see a liquid gleaming, a substance; I pick it up with a little spatula and take it to an analytic laboratory.

'Poison,' the biologist tells me.

'Poison…' I repeat.

My bee died of poisoning, it wasn't squashed. A few hours before, it had bitten me.

Who's going to keep my silences company? I miss the bee's buzzing, I need its soft whisper. And when the morning sun shines, I find my teeth clenched, and a sound coming from my mouth: zzzzzzzzzzzz...

*W*ere you ok yesterday? When you got home and lit yourself a cigarette from the gas ring in the kitchen, when our cat rubbed against your neck, breath quivering, when you shut your eyes and folded your legs like a foetus, what did you think about? Were you ok?

My torments began when I said goodbye to you at the airport, when I came over and said, 'So did you get all that? You check in, go up those escalators and then through the metal detector,' and I pointed to it with a finger, 'after which you go towards the gate marked on your boarding card, and you're there. Call me when you get home.'

That's what I said to you, and then I moved away, then came back and repeated it all word for word. I even repeated my gesture, pointing to the metal detector.

Finally I kissed you softly, our bodies apart, and whispered in your ear: 'Thank you.'

You, in a voice less harsh than mine, replied, 'Thank you, darling, thank you.'

That same evening I made love with Thomas. 'Let's do it as though it's the last time,' I said to him, looking him straight in the eyes.

He hesitated for a moment, then asked, 'What do you mean?'

'Don't be stupid… nothing apocalyptic. Just an excess of love.'

'Why?' he asked, dumbfounded.

I shrugged. 'Because I've had enough of giving myself away piecemeal. I need to stretch to infinity.'

'But you always do that,' he said.

I shrugged again and snorted.

No, I've never stretched to infinity. I don't know infinity. What I know is boundaries, paralysis, impairment. But no, not infinity.

'Let's do it this way. Imagine one of us dies tomorrow; imagine that one of us has to go travelling for years and years and then we had to each other again after a long time… or maybe never see each other again. How would you love me, how far would you go?'

He was extremely handsome, I was extremely beautiful. Warmed by the light from the lamp on the chest of drawers, which bathed our faces with specks of colour.

And when we made love he didn't exist, but he did exist and so did you. I existed, just an apparition. You and he loved me, tore me apart and kissed me. I saw your nose, his mouth, your ears and his eyes. I felt two hearts beating rather than one, and when my body surged I shouted, 'I love you so, so much,' and I was saying it to you as well.

You and he, guardians of my soul and my body. Presumptuously appearing on the terrace of my life, you watch and protect it as I have not asked you to, as I do not expect you to.

His sweat smelled like your neck, and his neck smelled of you. Then it was over. My eyelids lowered like the curtain after the show, and my soft, gratified breath merged with the smells of the room. And you stayed.

You've never made an attempt on my life or my liberty. You're so frail, and I'm too heavy. Now and again I'll have to silence all my theories of life to give more room to that extreme but gentle feeling I have for you.

Maybe you deserve that.

'A one-way ticket for Rome,' I said.

The man at the travel agency looked at me and smiled. 'Where are you off to this time?'

I looked at him for a moment, tracing every feature of his face inside my head.

'Home,' I replied.

He lowered his head as a sign of reverence and, looking furtively up at me, he said, 'Straight away.'

As he clicked away at the keys of his computer, I studied the brochures behind me. From the Congo to Laos, I could have gone anywhere. From Paris to Hokkaido. From Valparaiso to Athens. Endless possibilities spread out behind me, with many promises and few demands. I could have begun my escape straight away, since

I was there. But I was scared of the lack of responsibility, it's always frightened me.

'So you've decided on Rome?' the man asked.

I turned around and nodded with a smile.

'Do you want me to make you an electronic ticket?'

'No, please don't. I'd like to be able to hold it in my hand.'

It was like suddenly turning into the road I've seen so many times on the horizon from my street, the one I've been travelling down for such a short time, but I feel as though I've lived a hundred years already, half of those years spent well, the other half so-so, to put it optimistically.

It's always struck me as impossible to reach the point where the two roads cross, so that I've indolently travelled the whole journey without wondering where it would take me to and what I would do when I got there.

All of a sudden I've found myself at the turning into that unknown street, which a gilded sign identified as 'Likely Street. You can go straight on or choose to turn left.'

So I looked back and I saw my footsteps leading to the place where the parallel lines of the street joined in a perfect perspective: the tarmac was half-destroyed, ruined by hail, rain, the wind, cratered and worn to the thinnest of crusts. I saw trails of blood where people had fallen, here and there I saw corpses lying naked and gaping. No trace of you. Just hints of a mammalian smell that spread along the lifeless, deserted street. I took another look at the gilded sign: it looked like the entrance to paradise. But someone once told me that there is no better paradise than your own personal hell (or perhaps my conscience told me that, to give me an alibi?). In any case, I decided to tempt fate and, rather than continue along that grey street, which I reached by passing through a black hole shouting, 'Light! Light!' at the top of my voice, I sniffed the air and turned left, holding both hands crossed over my heart.

I took the airline ticket and held it delicately with two fingers: my ticket of entry.

As I left the agency, a thin line of cold made my skin ripple. I wrapped myself up in my coat (the red velvet one, the one Ornella thinks looks like a dressing-gown) and climbed the street called the Acchianata di San Giuliano. I decided to pass by Piazza Crociferi, where the excess and luxury of the baroque vie with the degradation, death and decomposition of those graffiti-scrawled houses, with flowers inexorably sprouting and withering from their stones. That's where I had my first kiss, where I came to blows with some halfwit, further over is the staircase where, one evening, I sipped a beer with a boy I didn't know, who didn't even ask for anything in return.

But no memory reawakened sensations that had been covered over by time.

So I went down, down as far as Piazza dell'Elefante, and all I saw was the grey coats of the council workers.

I walked on towards the fishmonger's, and even there the only thing that came to mind was that time many years ago when you, grandmother and I came here to buy fish; and the thing that struck me most that time had been the starfish on the back of the swordfish, which was still alive. A few, a very few memories, most of which are pointless and faded now.

If someone asked me which city I hated the most, I would say Catania. And I would give the same reply if they asked me which city I loved the most.

You've always told me that being far from your own land is the most painful thing imaginable. You've always told me that if and when I went away, I would feel homesickness grabbing me by the throat and dragging me down into a pit of sorrow and despair.

I told you that as far as I was concerned one place was pretty much the same as another, and that in fact Catania was the place I feared most, because Catania swallows people up.

Darkness, ash, lava cooled and congealed. In spite of the sun forever peeping among the baroque reliefs and the white lace curtains of the old houses in the centre, the whole city seems plunged in a big, endless, abysmal gloom. Catania is dark. It's as though it were sliding into a vast, gaping mouth, being pulled by an exhausted train. Catania's even like that when it seems that life can't be contained by its small squares and its stone-scratched streets, at night when young people, bag-snatchers, whores, drug addicts, families and tourists all arrange to meet in the same place, at the same time, leading to exotic, chaotic orgies. Catania is beautiful because it has no hierarchies, because it has no time, because it is unaware of its fascination. It is beautiful like a naked woman, white-skinned and with black, black hair, opening her eyes wide when a brute clamps his hand over her mouth, hissing, 'Don't breathe, you whore.'

That's what Catania is like, a whore who doesn't speak because someone is suffocating her.

I am a deeply Catanian creature. I have both life and death within me, I'm not afraid of either. But sometimes my life tends towards death.

Often I hear people who have been away from home for too long being told that the only thing drawing them back to their own bed is their need to take possession of their own roots, to eviscerate the earth and reappropriate their roots. Roots? What the fuck kind of roots are they talking about? We aren't trees, we're human beings. Human beings who have sprung from a seed, and remain seeds for all eternity. If anything, the only place we have ever put down roots is in the womb.

And, if one day I want to return to my origins, if I want to eat my roots, I'll just have to rip open your belly, climb in with my whole body, and bind myself to you with a cord that is nothing but a fiction now.

But it wouldn't do me any good. I want to go on being a seed. I want to be my origin and my end. And I don't want to rot in the ground, any ground, I want the wind to carry me for ever. I don't want ordered spaces.

⋆ 2 ⋆

*I*t isn't really spring yet, even if technically it is. The sky is still so wintry… and the faces of the people are wintry too. The Colosseum stands dramatically at the heart of the city, its fat arse in the middle of the road, exposed to everyone. I try as hard as possible not to look at it when I go shopping. I don't like the Colosseum, it looks like a middle-aged man trying to convince everyone of his virility, even though he lost it ages ago. I can't bear it. It wears me out. I walk down the noisy street, bags in hand and eyes lowered, I walk so fast that by the time I get to the front door my calves are hard and tense and my fingertips are sawn in half by the plastic bags; they look fat and swollen like a pack of sausages.

I suckled on the Catanian nipple for too short a time, perhaps I was weaned too soon. But it was what I asked for.

What did I do with all those years, in that dark, cramped chasm? How could I have failed to notice that

Catania was taking over my soul when I hadn't even granted it permission? Why didn't you tell me?

Did you conspire with the city to make me stay there for ever, clinging to your breasts? You constantly told me that I would be homesick for my city and my family, that if I went elsewhere I'd find loneliness and conflict, and that there's nothing finer than waking up in the morning and feeling the sea breeze stinging your nostrils. I don't care: I hate the sea and I'm really fond of loneliness and conflict.

Shame, though, that you got it wrong.

Sorry, I'm being harsh. I've always had a deviant vision of other people's thoughts; perhaps you didn't think all those things. But perhaps you hoped them, just a bit.

★ 3 ★

I didn't love him, I felt no tenderness for him, I wasn't particularly fond of him. I exploited his adulthood, his experience, the security he was able to give me.

He exploited the childish part of me that I guard so jealously, because it's small, insignificant, soft and yet precious. We exploited our bodies with the excuse that we were freeing our souls. He said I had given him my freedom, that with me he felt like a falcon. But what had he given me?

I gave myself to him because he was the only one at that point in time who could lick my wounds. Lick them, open them up and make them burn. And then lick them again.

I told myself that his body was exactly the same size as the deep abyss that had formed inside my own. I thought his body, stretched out on top of mine, might suddenly heal the bloody wound that opened up a little more each day, each day another centimetre.

Then I let him love me, and he let me love him.

At the precise moment when I came, I already felt sated and full, and wanted to be alone with myself. He turned his back on me and I curled up in a foetal position on the bed, closed in on myself. I masturbated.

Then he left me alone and stayed motionless on the unmade bed, completely naked, one arm over his head and his eyes fixed on the ceiling, lost in thought. His body still pulsed with erotic discharges, his virility a powerful presence.

In those moments of silent stillness, when the darkness of the hotel room was lit at intervals by the headlights of passing cars, I wondered what he would be left with if the natural perfume in which he was drenched was assimilated, swallowed, fixed within me. He would become an arid oak tree, about to die of dehydration, and his roots would be firmly planted in the earth, but the sap would no longer course through that rough and imposing trunk.

★ 4 ★

There's a sofa, and the pale blue light from the television screen. The sofa is covered with a pale fabric patterned with big brown flowers, and I'm wearing a tartan blanket. I'm four years old or maybe less. I've spent the whole day with my father, we've been watching the elections of the new president of the Republic. I haven't the faintest idea who he is, but Oscar Luigi Scalfaro is a nice name, it sounds pretty. It reminds me of my heroine, Lady Oscar. You're in bed with a headache; Dad soon joins you, and I'm left alone on the sofa, listening to the music of the cartoon, whispering, 'Lady Oscar, Lady Oscar, the blue of your eyes holds the rainbow... your sword... in battle... don't ever change, don't ever change... Lady Oscar...' My eyelids close heavily, I'm tired.

I fall into a deep sleep, not at all disturbed by the flashes from the television.

Someone is lying beside me, zapping the TV remote control.

An itch in my legs wakes me all of a sudden, my eyes are half-closed, and in a voice still thick with sleep I ask,

'What are you doing?'

Another voice replies, 'Don't worry, I'm just checking to see if you've become a lady.'

I go back to sleep, immersed in a field of brown flowers that Lady Oscar is elegantly felling with a clean sweep of her sword.

Blood drips from the stem of a flower.

<h1 style="text-align:center">★ 5 ★</h1>

I awake with a start, drenched in sweat, the sheet wrapped around my legs, I'm almost tangled, trapped as mosquitoes are trapped in tears.

Thomas is lying beside me, he's gone to sleep with his glasses on, and with *Il Manifesto* in his hand. I slip his glasses off, turn out the light and tell him I love him, lay my head on his chest and feel his heart squeaking, like a malfunctioning mechanism. Not regular, human beats, just a squeak, an attempt to stay alive. My first thought is this: until a few months ago, his heart would have exploded at contact with my face. Now it squeaks. What do you need, I wonder, the grease of love?

I was dressed as he liked. And I didn't mind going along with his aesthetic tastes and his desires: I was the one he desired. The fact that I liked him was neither here nor there, because pleasing him was the most important thing. We were sitting outside, at a restaurant just behind Piazza Teatro Massimo in Catania.

Summer was just over, and autumn was softening the faint tan that coloured my skin. The streets were calming down after the chaos that had become a constant lurking presence in the cobbled streets. The table stood at a slight angle in the uneven street. Reggae music filtered from the restaurant, and I couldn't help smiling when his face assumed an expression of amazement: I was well aware that this kind of music was as remote from him as it was possible to be. He would have preferred somewhere discreet, a place to which he could have applied adjectives like 'delicious', 'exquisite' or 'charming'. He would have called this place 'noisy', 'vulgar' and 'young'. But all he did was look at me and recoil from this place as best he could.

'It's extraordinary how you manage to make me say things that I've never said even to myself,' he said.

I just smiled. I wasn't listening to him.

'When I talk to you about my ruined dreams, about the new life you've given me, for the first time in my life I feel as though I'm not being judged. As though someone thinks highly of me. Do you understand what I'm getting at?'

I nodded. I looked utterly bored.

He stopped talking for a few minutes and then, gazing at me intensely, he asked, 'What do you think of me?'

The last thing a man should ever do is ask me what I think of him.

I don't think anything, what's to think? If I love you I love you, if you disgust me you disgust me. Is that so hard to figure out? And you want to know what I think? I think

you shouldn't give a fuck what people think of you. I think
you're selfish and cowardly, and blind, too. I think you were
so greedy for me that you didn't even feel, while you were
fucking me, that my body was as flat and motionless as the
expensive white wine in this big glass.

He looked at me with big eyes, like a whipped dog. He
waited.

I took a sip of wine and replied, 'I think you're a good
person.'

'You know, I've never felt free. Not even with my wife,'
he said, not paying the slightest attention to the words I
had just uttered.

I didn't feel like talking. He felt like talking. I let him go
on.

'I always have this vice around my heart, my brain and
my tongue, making me passive and powerless. Do you have
any idea what that means? Do you?' His voice had grown
reproachful, it was as though he was telling me off.

I shrugged and said gently, 'No, I don't know. I've
always loved my freedom.'

His lips trembled and he went on, more violently than
before. 'You're a little girl, and there are some things you
can't understand. You don't know what it feels like to be
deprived of yourself, to see your own dreams carried away
by rational, conscious, adult people! I was like you: I didn't
want to grow up, I felt free. But someone ripped me off.
And they'll rip you off too,' he said, clenching his teeth.

'That's one point of view,' I replied.

'You don't know a thing, you haven't a clue how I feel.'

No, and I don't want to know.

'I do know, Claudio. But please, don't keep going on at me about this.'

'What do you want to hear? That life is beautiful, that people love you, that it's all one long funfair?'

I smiled broadly and exclaimed, 'Why not?'

He started to cry, his voice growing muffled. Tears spilled from his eyes and trickled down the rough skin of his face.

I looked at him compassionately and whispered, 'Everything will be fine. We should go home, you've got to calm down.'

He nodded and moved away from the table without saying goodbye.

Left on my own, I went into the café and smiled as the music bounced off the walls.

A hundred times goodnight.

★ 6 ★

*H*is eyes were unsteady, they looked as though they were drenched with tears, they looked stunned, fragile, malleable. And yet they raped, they crushed, they pleaded, they reproached.

The parked car in a country lane at the feet of Etna, the rain that had finally stopped crashing against the windscreen, the smell of rotten earth, my panties and stockings scattered around inside the car, my hair heavy with damp, his penetrating breath and the smell of his aftershave. The tissues on top of the glove compartment, the colours of the purple, yellow and red flowers, the trucks passing behind our heads, the bee convulsively striking the window. Sweat, saliva and humours, the stench of damp fabric, the clink of his belt, the sun timidly reappearing, passion, haste, anxiety, jealousy, impotence, inconsistency, illusion, lies, indifference to the point of grief.

Everything was there, everything but love.

★ 7 ★

*M*y skin turned transparent. All of a sudden all my pores opened up until my body became one single great pore. My body like glass. My face too. My veins, my arteries, my capillaries. I can see everything. The red and purple motorways criss-crossing to form a beautiful cobalt blue. My ovaries are two little chickpeas suspended in mid-air. One is bigger and lower than the other, because of my period, which is due any minute. And then inside a red and lumpy pulp churns around like juice in a juice-dispenser. My kidneys are two beans, just as I imagined them when our teacher tried to explain their shape to us in primary school. I'm starting to think of my body as a vegetable garden. My lungs are coated with black moss, here and there, and the white splashes are rare now, rare but very beautiful.

My heart. My heart pulses, veiled by a nylon stocking, like the ones that bandits wear. A little condom with life inside it. A bandit on the run from death, but also from love and the extremity of pain. Because too much death has lain in wait for him, too much pain has buried him, too much love is strangling him.

My brain. My brain. My brain. Nothing but dreams. Many photographs and no sound.

When I was in the car with you and Dad, lots of things came into my head. I loved the car journeys we took, I liked driving all around the coast of Sicily, admiring the landscape that passed alongside us as infinite quantities of thought-molecules wrought havoc in my little brain. It was surprising how the coastline changed over a distance of only a few kilometres: from sand to cliffs, from cliffs to rock pools, sand again and then, unexpectedly, hills. A big, green hill ending in a sheer drop to the sea.

We set off early in the morning, and I woke first. I couldn't bear you waking me up, I didn't want to get in your way. So I got up and washed and by the time you woke up you already found me clean and neatly dressed. It was quite normal for you to find me already up and ready, you never paid me any special compliments. Perhaps if I had a child I would praise him, every now and again, just to make sure he didn't feel unwanted... to avoid making him feel incompetent, that's it. While Dad never even noticed what I was wearing, you studied me for minutes at a time.

'Why did you put on that skirt? It doesn't suit you, it needs washing.' 'What are you doing with those shoes? Going dancing? Put on a pair of trainers...wear the ones from last year, the dirty ones. We're going to the seaside, to

Grandma's, we're going to spend Easter there.'

And yet, on those trips, I felt fine. I left the window closed because I hated the wind filtering through the window of the moving car... it felt like a sword sent flying through the air, or a cowboy's lasso. I liked the sound of the radio, and I liked the sound of your voice when you spoke to Dad. From Mia Martini to Mina, from Riccardo Cocciante to Loredana Berté: those were the soundtracks to my thoughts. Those songs you used to sing at the top of your voice, the songs I learned by heart, whispering them shyly because I was ashamed of my hoarse, masculine voice. Loves shattered, lost, abandoned: those were the themes of my childhood. I often fell asleep. It was amazing, sleeping in the car, enclosed in an artificial belly kept alive by an engine. I almost felt as though I was returning to your womb. How did it feel to have me inside you? Did I feel like an intruder, or like part of you? Did I weigh that much? You've always been so small, so tiny... didn't having another life inside you hinder your movements? And did you ever talk to me? What did you say?

Only yesterday I asked Thomas to suck my breasts as though he was sucking milk. Lately I've been feeling maternal all the time. Anything that makes me feel like a woman is a blessing.

Seriously: you know what I thought during those long, long journeys? I thought, 'One day I'd like to publish a diary, I'd like to write about my life. I must seriously think about keeping one...even if I know I would soon tire of writing.'

One day I asked Dad to give me a nice diary with a lock. For a week, every day when he came home, I asked him, 'Dad, have you got the diary?' I always asked him when we were having our dinner, always in a low voice, and I asked him when the table was already plunged into silence, I didn't want to interrupt you. Each time I asked him if he had brought the diary I felt guilty. When he said, 'No,' I wasn't angry: it was the most obvious answer to such an indiscreet question. If he had brought one home, he would have given it to me straight away; what was the point in my asking?

Weeks later you took me with you in the car, you let me out and we went into the tobacconist's. The skeletal lady behind the counter, the one with the boiled-fish eyes and the fine, fine hair, was the mother of one of my classmates in primary school: I liked her, she was like a fairy dressed up as a witch. All my schoolmates were afraid of her, while I thought she was actually beautiful. You pointed towards a shelf with notebooks, pencils, pens and other kinds of writing equipment; a diary had been thrown in the middle. The cover was smooth and white, a dirty white, with a picture of a blonde girl in a leather jacket sitting on a motorbike. The diary was very thin, there couldn't have been more than twenty pages in it. And the padlock looked extremely fragile, golden and covered with little brown stains. It was the only one they had. It was a leftover from the '80s. I was extremely happy, and although it was horrible I absolutely loved it. The fairy disguised as a witch charged you 1,500 lire for it.

But my usual capriciousness soon led me to abandon the project. I wrote only five pages before I got tired.

'I'll write when I can't help saying something,' I promised myself. I hated having to write anything meaningless.

So, when I thought the moment had come to bury my soul and keep only my material alive, pure and lewd, some perverse angel whispered in my ear, 'Write. These emotions will never return. If you write, a scrap of soul will be left in your breast.'

And because I have never had anything to lose, in pretending to keep a diary I wrote a novel.

★ 8 ★

This evening as he laughed I noticed that one of his teeth overlapped with another, as though shyly hiding. I found this defect incredibly fascinating, and wondered for what strange reason I had never noticed it before. I know his moles, his skin, I know the different smells that arise one by one from the exploration of his body. I know that he has an extra rib, the one he didn't give to the woman. He has freckles on his back and big, deep knuckles on his hands. The gleam of the stars is a flat, monotonous glare in comparison with the flash of his eyes. He has a soft mouth, the kind only women tend to have. He has a maternal belly and breasts, soft as the limbs of a newborn child.

He has a mole under his eye, in the same place as mine.

As I looked in delight at that twisted tooth, he stared at me and asked, almost irritably, 'What's up?'

I knew something was wrong.

I knew I was about to be abandoned.

The first thing we shared was a book of poems by
Mao Tse Tung, bought in an antiquarian bookshop. We
read it at night, in his room, our warm, naked bodies
covered by the duvet. Red Christmas lights hung from the
walls of the room, and we thought we were in a
transparent cube suspended in mid-air, from which we
could be seen by anyone.

⋆ 9 ⋆

They put us outside beneath a damp, watery sky. All we had to shelter us was a few umbrellas, gas heaters our sole source of warmth. A very bright light was angled towards our table, and the smoke from the roasting meat clung insolently to our hair.

I wanted to go, I wondered what the hell I was doing there.

'Meeting important people', that's what my condition means I have to do. But my mind and body mutiny.

As far as I'm concerned, the people sitting around this table, assailed by the damp and the smell of roasting meat, aren't important. I couldn't give a toss about this actor, that editor can go fuck himself, thank you very much, that photographer can squash herself into one of her own pictures and live inside it for ever.

Because this is what all we human beings do: we stay trapped inside our creations, our worlds. And no one can save us from our worlds, no one can drag us out of them.

And while they all raise their glasses to my success and a thousand more to come, I repeat just one thing in my head: 'Go fuck yourselves, the lot of you, you horrible arse-licking cunts. I'd just like to see the look on your faces if I showed you my pussy.'

And I grip Thomas's hand as I whisper to him, 'Take me away from here, now.'

⋆ 10 ⋆

I'm eating salted crackers, over there some delirious jazz pours from the stereo, and outside it's raining. My hips are so wide that you can rest your elbows on them.

My voice is hoarse. Massimiliano was here this morning, that Neapolitan friend I told you about a few times: sometimes he comes to see me and when he smiles I can't tell if he's sad or what.

'I'm frightened,' I whispered to him.

He looked at me compassionately, embarrassed, and said, 'Of what?'

'I'm frightened that he might betray me…' I replied.

'What makes you think that?'

'Nothing… it's just a feeling.'

He looked at me and nodded, and I immediately understood what he was thinking.

I screwed up my eyes as tightly as I could and screamed, 'Do you think I'm crazy?'

He said I was getting reality muddled up, that the world I thought I lived in wasn't the real world.

'Open your eyes, Melissa. You're creating a reality that has nothing to do with the reality around you.'

I took him by one arm and hurled him out with such violence that a scrap of his checked shirt stayed in my hand, torn out by my furious fingers.

Then I shut the door behind him and felt dizzy for a moment. Exhausted, I went to the bathroom and noticed that in my haste I had left a blood-filled sanitary towel in the basin. It doesn't matter, blood doesn't bother anyone. I went out on to the balcony; the washing machine had finished its cycle. I stood and looked inside the drum for a while, I don't know why. My head is so full of thoughts that it seems empty. I'm sated with happiness, happiness is exhausting me, demoralising me. I ask myself every day, every moment, if this happiness will come to an end and when that will be. I'm too apocalyptic, I know. And maybe masochistic. Yes, I'm well aware of that. The messages sent by the world are exasperating: nothing lasts for ever, everything comes to an end, everything withers, everything dies. And if it didn't happen to me, well what about that? If I stayed this age for ever, if I remained intellectually ignorant, if I stayed in love for ever, what about that?

I know, I can't accept change, I'm too much of a traditionalist, too attached to my memories and, paradoxically, attached to fantasies about the future. That's why my present is so restless, even if it's happy: I mix the past, the future and the present as though an exquisite sweet might emerge from the dough. A sweet that does you good because it hurts. A sweet that is good because it is full of warring ingredients.

There is nothing positive in this wealth of feelings. It's an orgy, Mamma. An orgy of feelings. In which it's impossible to work out who's winning, in which you can't predict whether the ultimate winner will be death or life, love or pain. It's an infinite chaos, bound by many little interlocking rings that have slipped into my throat, dragging me to places that are never the same, to more and more exasperating states of mind.

I'm disturbed to the depths of my marrow. I don't know how to hold back my instincts, I allow myself to be corrupted by my obsessions, by my most violent passions. Do you think it's just because I'm Sicilian? Or could it be because I'm fucking terrified of losing the most beautiful part of me? Of losing Thomas?

⋆ 11 ⋆

I shook him awake, I was breathless.
'There are ghosts, I can hear them,' I whispered so they couldn't hear me.

A dream, he said, a bad dream, calm down, he said.

No, I couldn't. I really did hear that hand striking the wall opposite the bed. It beat out a rhythm, giving it a sweet melody. And through half-open eyes I had seen a tall, black female figure.

Go to sleep, go to sleep, don't be afraid. Go to sleep, go to sleep, don't be afraid. Don't be afraid.

This morning the memory of the night has already passed, but a strange attraction leads me to long once more for the black darkness. I hear a weird echo, I sip the careless milk of my thoughts, my legs are naked and crossed, I look impatiently at my cigarettes, because seven hours without smoking is far too long.

The stench of the dirty dishes in the sink grows from day to day, this morning I decide to clean the house, I swear I'm going to do it. I'm serene, even if that echo sounds like a Tibetan chant that won't leave me alone, but doesn't bother me either.

He says, 'Come and see.'

I go and look with my lips open in a smile, across the narrow corridor, and I think and feel that this morning I really do feel like making love. I think that when I go into the room I'll throw him on the bed and fuck him without even looking at him. He's just had a shower and he's damp, I can already feel the skin of his feminine back brushing against my fingertips.

'Come and see,' he repeats.

I don't go in, I stop in the doorway, with one leg against the wall and a smile that hints broadly at what I have in mind.

He doesn't notice, but points at the wall with a finger.

A black hand. Or rather not a hand, three fingers. Three black fingers imprinted on the wall, as though someone had set fire to his own skin and then pressed it against the plaster.

I just say, 'I told you so,' and feel something clenching inside me, and someone tells me that I have to hide because no one knows how to listen to that echo.

⋆ 12 ⋆

I realised I was in love with him one late summer
evening. An electric evening, in a Rome that was
colder than usual, turned in on itself as though to apologise
for making too much noise, for being too beautiful, too
schizophrenic, too old. The Rome of emperors and
usurers, of politicians and tax-collectors, lost girls and girls
in miniskirts and stilettos, the Rome of wines and dairies,
churches and brothels.

Sipping my Vin Santo, I studied the images running
across the screen. The TV enfolded and contained me, and
for the first time the eyes and words of the scarecrow
presenters were directed at me, like rough-edged swords
waiting to be used. What was I like? I wasn't. I wasn't me.
I was the caricature of myself, I was the most exasperating
version of myself, I said all the things I would never have
wanted to say, because what I want to say is too crazy and
too confused for anyone to understand. I was only
pretending to be able to cope.

Martina and Thomas were lying on a big leather sofa,
Simone and I had our eyes glued to the TV.

'Tommy, would you give my back a rub? I'm aching like a beast…' said Martina.

He brought his cigarette to his mouth and held it tightly between his lips, letting it dangle. He kept his eyes half-closed, to shield himself from the smoke that brought tears to his eyes; his long eyes, with their almost girlish lashes, looked even longer, two crescent moons.

Martina turned her back to him, and he started rubbing her vertebrae with two fingers, strong and extremely delicate. I thought about how good it must be to have two big hands like those on your body, and the smoke from his cigarette filling my nostrils. At that moment I desired him, and not just physically.

At some point I even thought of asking him, 'Thomas, would you rub my back too?' and I swear I nearly did.

But I don't know how it happened…

That very evening, on an enormous Empire-style bed, Claudio lay on top of me and I half-heartedly opened my legs. By now I was wearing nothing but a black silk bra.

The smell of old wood gave me a comforting sense of warmth. The darkness engulfed everything. I was wearing the necklace with the pearl that you gave me, the only spark of light in the room. My thoughts were like long, long shooting stars whose tips I couldn't find. Claudio's attitude towards me was a mixture of jealousy and envy, and if I didn't dedicate enough time to him he was hurt and made me feel guilty. He cried on the phone, begging me not to leave him, mortifying my happiness. 'I can't wait for this dust-cloud to settle,' he said, 'I want to have you all to myself. And don't kid yourself, they'll forget about you soon enough.'

No, Claudio, I'm not kidding myself. I hope deeply that they do forget me, I hope no one remembers me. And you, Claudio, you've got to forget me too.

Claudio entered me and started moving back and forth. I felt my swollen belly, and felt his penis as something strange now, something unfamiliar. I turned my head to one side as I felt his abdomen rubbing against my pubic bone.

With my nipples erect I wanted to torture him.

After five or six thrusts he usually started sweating, water pouring from his forehead. When he was on top of me, the drips ran along his face and reached my lips, and I licked them wearily away with my tongue: they were very salty and bitter, with a vague taste of sperm.

That night he didn't get as far as perspiration, because at the third thrust I stopped him and said, 'I'm in love with someone else, I can't do this.'

He broke away from me without a word, and I turned to face the other side of the bed. In front of me there was a huge mirror framed in an old wardrobe, and I stared at myself for a few moments that felt like an eternity. I studied myself and saw once again that same lost, passive expression that has accompanied me throughout my life.

'You aren't in love with someone else, you're in love with your success, and you think I'm a hopeless fool who's barely capable of satisfying your whims,' he whispered a few minutes later.

'Please stop,' I whispered, tired of hearing him say that success had altered me. The only thing that had changed was his vision of me, I felt that he was hostile, and that he now saw me as something that belonged not to him but to everyone. I was starting to despise him. Not to hate him, but to despise him.

'It's the writer you met at that party, isn't it?'

'If that's what you want to think, go ahead and think it,' I replied indifferently, 'I'm stupid as always… I always tell you everything. But things are going to change from now on, you'll see,' I said, facing away from him and speaking in a very quiet voice.

I heard him crying, but shut my eyes. I couldn't have cared less about his victimhood.

He just cried for a while, and soon worked out that it wasn't going to move me. His tears flowed whenever he needed someone to give him a little understanding.
I wished him black with bruises from my fists, white from my withheld caresses. With my nipples erect, I wanted to torture him.

The sheets rustled a little, and before I worked out what was happening I heard a croak coming from his mouth.
I looked into the mirror in front of me, which showed the figure behind me, and could quite clearly see the sheet which was slightly raised, and his hand gripping his penis.

He was masturbating in bed next to me, partly in order to come, but also partly, perhaps, to take his revenge on me.

I felt him touching himself and shut my eyes, I tried to sleep and feel nothing more.

With my nipples erect, I wanted to torture him.

He got up and went to the bathroom, from where I heard his final, long moan of pleasure.

The next morning we had breakfast in silence. I never saw him again.

In a sense I felt like an orphan, although one with two fathers: a natural one for whom I have never felt anything, not rancour, or rage, or love; and one whom I had taken it upon myself to love, and on whom I had imposed the task of loving me.

With my nipples soft, freedom arrived.

★ 13 ★

I'm naked at the computer, he's in the kitchen washing the dishes and whistling. I like noise when I'm writing, I like a racket. Then he puts on a CD and I, still writing, find myself moving my hips and making my revolving chair move back and forth. The curtains aren't closed yet and the windows are high, typical of a seventeenth-century palazzo. Everybody can see us, but we're happy for anyone to see us making love, and perhaps that's typical of people in love: showing everyone you love each other. I wander along the corridor, brushing the walls with my fingers, I go into the sitting room and stroke the bonsai tree, standing on tiptoes. He has his back to me, I wrap my arms around his chest and start rubbing my pelvis against him. I turn him resolutely round, look at him coyly, aware that I've made a movement he liked. I turn around, rub my buttocks against him, and he delicately strokes my back; I sit down on the edge of the cold, wet sink, the contact makes my whole skin shiver, and my body swells upwards.

He takes me there and then, grandiosely stretches his

body out on top of mine and whispers words I like into my ear, warming my earlobe with his breath.

Then I hear a coughing fit and open my eyes: I see a woman leaning over the table, coughing convulsively, she looks up and smiles wickedly at me. She's blonde, wearing a flower-patterned dress, she's thin and coarse. I look at her for a moment longer, then I look at him, close my eyes, open them again, look back at the woman and see that she's disappeared. I can still hear her coughing. I draw him towards me and devour him.

His tongue bleeds, dripping red on my neck.

⋆ 14 ⋆

*L*ovely, absolutely lovely, that film was fantastic.
A touch of genius in that shot.

And what do you think of the new director in competition at the Berlin festival? And Cannes? And Venice?

Well…I…

And what do you think about Edgar Allan Poe, about Céline, about the fin-de-siècle decadent poets? Don't you think their words blend perfectly with their ideas?

Yes, of course…but…

And did you see the Paul Klee exhibition? And the Tintoretto? Did you see Tarantino's latest, and Buñuel's first?

No…

Your brains are in a state of collapse. You all know how to know. I don't.

I'm a homo sapiens who hasn't evolved yet. I'm still in the initial phase and I intend to stay there.

They're all motionless pillars of ash. Compacted ash, impossible to break. I'd so love to walk on their soot. Their stillness frightens me, yet at the same time I'm fascinated by it.

Someone once said that we're surrounded by dead people. Dead people walk in the street, eat, drink, make love and read lots of books and see lots of films and know lots of important people. But dead people, unlike living people, can't have palpitations, they can't have emotions. They use only their intellects, their minds, and they tend to show off their own culture.

I'm scared of dead people.

I'm scared of the thought that maybe, one day, I might die too.

At the beach at Roccalumera there was an enormous sign bearing the words NO SWIMMING, and yet it was the most crowded beach in the whole of eastern Sicily. There was no sand, there were no rocks. Just pebbles. Pebbles that got stuck between your toes, that dug into your tender skin.

'Here, put your rubber shoes on so it won't hurt.'

But I've always hated those horrible rubber shoes. They made me feel ugly, they made me feel like one of those old German tourists with little white hats and those inevitable rubber ballet-shoes on their feet.

I preferred to hurt myself, and when I did a lot of walking I even ended up liking that sensation, that gentle torture that I inflicted on my childish skin.

I didn't like going down to the beach in the morning, the ideal time for me was early afternoon, straight after lunch.

'You can't go swimming, not right after lunch,' you,

Grandma and my aunts all chorused. While the men inside snored, back from their night's fishing.

'No, I swear, I'm not going to go swimming, I'm going to lie down in the sun,' I said seriously.

'You'll get sunstroke!'

'I'll wet my head every now and again,' I replied wisely.

I set off with all the paraphernalia, accompanied by Francesco and Angela, who had previously dispatched me on an expedition to persuade you to let us go.

We crossed the street, the three of us hand in hand, and once we reached the shore we threw the lilo into the water and lay down on it. We played at betting who would get their belly wet first. The water was extremely cold and it felt as though all the food we had just consumed was freezing in our stomachs. After our first unpleasant experiences, we had also grown used to jellyfish. Around here they're small but deadly. We brought olive oil, Nivea cream and butter. We mixed it all up together and spread it over the place where we were stung which, in contact with these substances, fried like bacon and eggs. Then we put a hot stone on top, gritted our teeth and beat our feet on the ground.

Francesco, small as he was, managed to impale the jellyfish with his dagger. At the water's edge there were dozens of decomposing jellyfish, melting in the sun and giving off steam.

While he was cruelly killing jellyfish on the beach, Angela and I ran in under the shower, sure that no one could see us. We let the water run over us and sang the theme tune from a television music programme: 'Brancamen-ta! Ta-ra-ta-ta...', writhing like snakes in a bowl.

You all arrived at about five o'clock. From a distance, washed out by the sultry air, you looked like characters from a Sergio Leone film. The heat, the silence all around, you armed with your fighting-gear: sunglasses, cushions for your backs, hairbands, eye-masks, sarongs, transistor radios, Tupperware containers full of biscuits, fruit and panini made with oil, tomato and salt. My favourites, the ones that stung my chapped lips.

We looked at one another from a distance and felt like thoughtless beasts, instinctively assessing an opponent's weak points. After a few minutes you started running and shouting at us, 'You scoundrels, you've been swimming, haven't you!'

'Eight wasted years! You're eight years old and you've wasted them all!'

'I'll have your soul, you wicked child!'

'Mamma, how are you going to take my soul?'

It seemed a lovely image, you making a hole in my stomach and pulling out my soul with your hands, as though it was a rope.

We felt an exponential joy: the joy of our aquatic play, and the joy of transgressing your stupid rules. Why... if you didn't want us to go swimming after eating, why on earth did you bring food to the beach?

At seven o'clock, when the sun started shrinking and the sea turned grey, down came the Boss.

The Boss was no taller than us children; she had short
fair hair, big green eyes, her skin was smooth as silk and her
breasts were worn out by having six children in as many
years, her belly swollen and hard. And her thighs… the
most beautiful thighs I have ever seen. Slender and sleek,
without a hint of cellulite, toned and soft.

The Boss came down to the beach even more heavily
armed than you, with jars of water, trays full of food, boxes
of ice creams and big bunches of bananas. The Boss filled
us with awe, and we children were forced to eat the
bananas beneath her gaze.

'Eat it up for your *Nonna*, it'll do you good.'

Our stomachs were endless storehouses of food, we
could have kept going for months. It was her way of
expressing her affection.

At the eighth banana, if one of us said, 'That's enough,
Grandma, I'm full,' she cast you a glance so grim that you
wet yourself, and it was a good thing our suits were wet
already. Then down came Dad and my uncles, with their
own gear: cameras and movie cameras. They said they
wanted to photograph us children, but in actual fact their
lenses were always trained on the bottoms of the women in
the sea. You got furious, but still you took the sun,
mumbling, 'What's so lovely about that bum, what do they
see in it? It's flabby, sagging…'

Every weekend the band came and set up in the central
courtyard surrounded by the villagers' houses. I watched it
all, sitting on the concrete step, letting my legs dangle
because I couldn't touch the ground with my feet. There

was Signor Sibilla who, when his wife went away, flirted with his neighbour, a fat, vulgar woman who gave off a strong, rancid smell. Then there was the Witch, who came down covered in sequins, her eyes surrounded by gleaming, green eye-shadow, her black, black hair down to her shoulders, always wearing tight, fluorescent clothes. She sat down next to the band's keyboard player and tried to follow the music so that she could play the songs on her pianola the next day. She was our band for the rest of the week.

Grandma's thighs, on these occasions, were sublime as she danced 'Put your hands in the air, shake them all about… Do it when Simon says, and you will never be out'.

They were sublime both to me and to Signor Loy, the Sardinian who looked like a tarantula. Every weekend the band had to leave earlier than planned because Grandad started punching Signor Loy who, undaunted, went on slobbering over Grandma.

Queen of the summer, she was more radiant than the rest. She gleamed, and her brilliance was more powerful than the sun's reflection. More glittering than the Witch's sequins.

★ 15 ★

Sometimes I think about you. No, that's not true, not sometimes: I think about you all the time. And every time I do a tear slips out, from only one eye. If Thomas asks me why I'm crying I reply that it's nothing, that I've focused my eye on a point on the horizon, and that's why my iris is stinging. I'm thinking about you and your unbroken solitude.

The pizza has just turned up, you've been searching through the money box to find coins, because the boy has no change. When he (and his pimples) have disappeared, you laugh and say, in Sicilian dialect, 'Che scemu carusu' – 'What a stupid boy.'

You sit down on the sofa with your legs crossed and switch on your television, trying to find a film that might move you. A costume drama, preferably, with a tight, romantic plot. Francesco and Morino are sniffing at the tomato on your pizza, you hold out a glob of sauce on one finger. You've already opened the windows, the terrace with the little garden is a few feet away, you catch the freshness of the newly watered lawn. It's lovely to see

Ornella lying on her belly on the carpet, head on a cushion, face pointing straight at the TV. But her eyelids are closed, she's just gone to sleep.

I love hearing her tell you to fuck off when you call her to go to bed, to get between the sheets. She rises to her feet, looks at you with her direct, imperious eyes and says, 'You're a fucking idiot, why the hell did you wake me up?'

You don't reply, because if you did the two of you will come to blows.

If I'd been with you, I would have sat still with my cheek pressed against your bum, and would soon have gone to sleep. But now you're alone and the cats have followed Ornella between the sheets.

You've lit a cigarette, and sat yourself down in front of the television. Your eyes, which are made of water, are drowning in an ocean of tears.

When you wake up, you realise that it wasn't my voice calling you, but the infuriating crackle of the umpteenth unextinguished cigarette, making the umpteenth hole in the same old sofa.

You go to bed, knowing that I wasn't calling you, and you won't be able to get pissed off and say, 'What the hell do you care if I sleep here on the sofa?'

You slink off to bed, tears drying on your cheeks.

And I'm in another world, falling in love.

I think about me, about you, about him, about me and him, especially. Your eyes are made of water, mine of fire, his of earth. Out of the three, I'm the one who can endure your dominion, the one who loves it.

⋆ 16 ⋆

I advanced, slowly at first and then, once I had
managed to touch his thigh with my knees, my
movements became even more enveloping. I circled him
lightly with an arm. His body stiffened and his breath
seemed to falter for a few moments. He stayed motionless,
blocking off all contact with the world. With my
outstretched little finger I gently touched his erection. It
was powerful, yet incredibly light. I had never touched a
real erection before. That was why my hand moved higher
and higher until it reached his heart. When he lightly
brushed my fingers, I realised that nothing would be as
before.

'Do you want to sleep with me tonight?' I asked him.

We were at Cosenza in Calabria, and the university
where I was staying had put two rooms at my disposal, one
for me and the other for my companion.

'It's horrible sleeping on your own…' I went on,
plunging further and further into my embarrassment.

'Ok,' he replied, his cheeks growing fiery.

The smell of his neck was intoxicating, he was young,

he was a child. He was everything I wanted.

'The sweet scent of your breath…' he whispered suddenly in the night, 'I love the sweet scent of your breath.'

I clutched his T-shirt with my fingers and closed my eyes.

He imprisoned my breath in a glass jar, and he sniffs it every time he makes love with me.

★ 17 ★

*T*he train's progress accompanies our movements, our sighs creating a light and liquid counter-melody, with sudden surges of emotion, our lips brushing, a race to kiss each other's bodies, tongues darting disturbingly, imperiously, the night's darkness, broken here and there by streetlamps scattered along country roads, reconciling troubled fantasies and provocative imaginings, my thighs gripping his body, pressing him tightly and crying out to him, 'You'll never want to go! Why are you getting away? Why won't you come back? Why won't you suck my breath?'

The palms of my hand against his warm, maternal body, my neck thrown back, my eyes holding back their tears, perhaps tears of blood.

The echo has started whispering in my head again, too faint to be properly understood, but loud enough for me to perceive a breath of wind, the north wind. All of a sudden I came, giving off so much energy that he too felt an electric shock in his belly. Blood, blood everywhere. Blood in my head, blood in my eyes. Empty, my veins.

Then I trace a line with the fountain pen my father gave me, the one I use to write with, I want to work out whether I've still got any blood inside me. Empty, completely empty.

I just remember him going back to his cabin and shouting. I remember his dirty fingers and his forlorn and distant eyes.

And distance, one day, will take him to the very rim of the segment of our life, he will go far from me and end up in Her arms. When he is with Her, mists will rise up and thicken, and keep him from remembering. While he is with her, I will die slowly, allowing myself to be dragged along with those mists. That way at least I'll see him from close to.

A poisonous tapeworm nests in our bellies; the slides of our life are printed on its body. Each time the tapeworm moves, and slide settles on our navel, and the light projected outside enchants us. We stand and stare at it, then we burst into tears.

At first I couldn't work out what it was that stirred in my belly. I thought it was a child that didn't want to grow and didn't want to be born, a child that wanted to stay immersed and suspended in my amniotic fluid. But then I saw images in my head, and those images were born of pain.

And that pain was born of the movements of my entrails, my guts, my flesh.

A pain with its own roots in my past, and I can't cough that past away: I have to live it, and I have to watch it.

The tapeworm helps me do that, the tapeworm loves me.

⋆ 18 ⋆

*T*he sea was rough and I was four years old and wearing a red costume. The beach was scorched by the early afternoon sun, the pebbles gleamed and stood out against the intense blue of the sky. Around my waist I had a plastic rubber ring with a pattern of red apples. I held it up with both hands, stamping my feet because I wanted to swim at all costs, even though the waves seemed determined to swallow everything up.

'I want to swim!' I shrieked, tears pricking my eyes.

My father, lying on his mat, pretended not to hear me.

'I want to swim!' I repeated until he was forced to look up and look at me impatiently.

'Well you can't,' he said, 'the sea's too rough.'

'That's what I like about it,' I replied, 'I like playing with the waves.'

Lying on your stomach and sunning your back, you muttered, 'Go on, let her do it, go on, as long as you're there nothing will happen.'

Inside I was smiling with satisfaction, but my face was still furious.

I ran towards the water's edge, still holding up my rubber ring. Dad caught up with me, I put one foot into the water and it was terribly cold, but I didn't care.

'It's cold,' he said, 'let's get out.'

I said nothing, but just kept walking until the water came halfway up my belly.

I headed towards the open sea, my toes no longer touching the bottom, and now the waves were dragging me and my rubber ring. Behind me, Dad was getting impatient with me saying, 'Dad, let's go.'

I swam and played with the waves that buoyed me, high and majestic. Perhaps I was smiling. They were like big arms that lifted me up and then dropped me back down again, and for a moment I felt a mixture of fear and delight. Fear of drowning and delight at being lifted towards the sky, just for a moment, just for a second. I felt myself being rocked.

I turned around and saw him, so impatient now that his face was almost contorted with pain.

I felt so much sorrow at that moment, I saw his wet trunks and I thought it was bad that he was feeling cold. I saw the pained expression on his face, and felt so much tenderness, I chastised myself for being selfish, for thinking about my games.

'Dad, let's go back to the shore.'

He practically ran out of the water, while I floundered impetuously, battling against the waves that seemed more and more intent on carrying me out to sea.

With my eyes narrowed slightly, I tried to get closer to

him, but I couldn't. I still said nothing, because I didn't want to see that expression on his face, I had to do it on my own.

By the time I reached the shore, he was already lying on his mat reading the paper.

★ 19 ★

*L*ast night I had a beautiful, disturbing dream. I was in it, with Thomas and a little girl. A beautiful little girl with red hair, a round face and a pair of red, fleshy lips. I was almost frightened at the sight of her, her beauty was disconcerting. She was our daughter.

But in the dream I was at once myself, and Thomas, and the girl. I could see with everyone's eyes. I felt part of everyone.

We were dressed in nineteenth-century clothes. Not the sumptuous nineteenth century of the courts, but the nineteenth century of the ordinary villagers.

The little girl takes us to the sea. She makes us immerse ourselves in the waves, but we don't swim.

We stay suspended under the water for a long time. Around us there are octopus, jellyfish, lobsters… The little girl is lying suspended above the void, her arms along her hips and her long, long red hair still growing and flowing beneath the water. Her hair is beautiful and silky, and it grows and grows. Then, at some point, her hair turns white and bristly, and starts to shrink back until it finally disappears. Now her head is bald. She's a newborn baby. But she is still surprisingly beautiful.

I kiss her, I press her to my breast, and she shuts her eyes and lays her face on my neck. An icy sensation woke me up. I touched my neck and it was extremely cold. But all that lasted only a few seconds because I shut my eyes again and went on with my dream. The little girl has died in my arms and I have floated to the surface, passing through a cave. Thomas stays down there, looking at her and kissing her. But I have left only in a physical sense because I'm still seeing through Thomas's eyes. He picks up the little girl, rises to the surface and, when he reaches the cave, he lifts her into the air and cries, 'She's alive! She's alive!'

You, dressed all in black, run and shout with joy. I go on looking at her beautiful face, and realise that she isn't alive at all. She's dead. But I pretend she's alive. We all pretend she's breathing.

One day I will inhabit my dreams, and have a great orgy of love with all the people I love, all the people I have loved.

★ 20 ★

'Do you want to?' the man asked me.

He was tall, quite sturdy, with two burning black eyes and curly black hair that thinned over his forehead.

He was holding out a half-open wooden box, in the other hand he held a 100 Euro note and a slim box-cutter.

I stared at him and imagined that he was the chief of an African village, offering me the treasure of his land, while with the other hand he was handing me the sacrificial dagger with which I was to cut my finger and mingle my blood with his.

'It's really good, excellent stuff,' he went on.

I imagined the men of the village digging the dark, dry earth to remove that precious, crystalline material.

He gestured to me to accept his gift.

I stared into his eyes, I saw he wasn't really there. He saw me, but he wasn't looking at me.

He wasn't fully in control of his faculties, and he didn't understand that he was looking at a little girl who was barely of legal age, and who looked at least four years younger than she really was.

I shook my head.

He smiled at me and tipped his powder on to a silver tray, splashed here and there with a few drops of champagne. He wiped away the droplets with the cuffs of his shirt and muttered something.

All of a sudden he sniffed. He raised his head and threw it back and closed his eyes, twitching his nose like a rabbit.

For a moment I thought I saw his body turning transparent, I saw his skin melting, and his internal organs becoming visible. They were darker than his eyes, and here and there the mucous membrane was torn by an ulcer. The crystal powder spread all the way through his body, branching like a river into different streams, and it looked almost like a divine spring, a purifying fountain.

Then a large belly appeared, followed by the rest of the body of a beautiful woman who walked over to African-chief-guy and stroked his hair, asking him if it was good.

He took a deep breath, widening his nostrils, and replied, 'Divine.'

The woman pulled a face, as though to say, 'A shame I've got a brat in my belly, otherwise…'

Then she looked at me and asked me, 'You've never tried it, have you?'

I shook my head and answered, 'No, I don't like it.'

She nodded, walked towards a big chest of drawers, opened one of the drawers and took out a joint, already rolled.

She looked at it as I might look at a particularly fine penis, and then she sighed.

She lit it and lay back on the bed, smoking with gusto.

A few weeks later I saw her acting in a film, her hair was longer and she didn't have the belly yet. Her pupils were tiny pinpricks.

* 21 *

It happened all at once. I was sitting on the toilet, and felt first an itch in my ovaries and then a dull splash in the toilet bowl. When I was little I was convinced that frogs could come out of the toilet and climb up my back. I lifted myself up from the bowl, holding my legs wide, and blood dripped to the floor.

There were no frogs in it. There was a tadpole. A human tadpole. It was red, floating in a golden swimming pool, looking at me with its one black eye, which was almost bigger than its own head. With a little tail, its body was elongated like a lizard's.

'*Suttu 'n palazzu c'è 'n cani pazzu, te pazzu cani stu pezzu ri pani*,' this disgusting creature whispered, a tongue-twister in the Sicilian dialect of my childhood.

I felt my heart tremble and my mind growing fogged. It swam there, moving back and forth as though enjoying its aquatic game. I could hear the shrill laughter of a child in the distance, and that tadpole went on swimming and swimming, repeating its curious phrase.

Then, afraid that it was a monster, I flushed the toilet.

A mighty whirlpool dragged it down to the sewer.

Because of the noise of the water I didn't hear Thomas arriving. He had closed the door, and was putting his bag on the ground.

'I'm home!'

Grabbed him. That's what I should have done. Grabbed him and strangled him.

'Where are you hiding?'

Strangled him with rage, with keen love, with the love that made me love him for an infinitesimally short space of time and the death that he dragged from my belly.

'*Pequeña*…where are you?'

I came out of the toilet, looking at the floor, and smiled at him.

'What were you doing?' he asked.

'I was in the toilet,' I replied.

Lick away the blood and hold him naked and clean under the pillow.

'Hey, listen, I've brought you a surprise…!' he said enthusiastically.

Touch his soft limbs and plunge a finger into his chest. Rip out his heart and lift it to the sky.

'I know it took two of us, but I put up no resistance…'

Attach him to my nipple for a few minutes, long enough to weep.

Then I felt a hairy head stroking my calves, and for a moment I thought my son had returned in the form of a velvety ghost.

I looked straight ahead of me and asked Thomas,

'What is it?'

He stared at me and then he said, 'It's a dog...'

I lowered my head, eyes full of tears.

And then I burst out crying and screaming.

The darkness had already entered the room, the red curtain floated slightly in the wind, while the noise from our neighbours' TV filled the still silence.

'What shall we do?' he asked me, stroking my feet.

'He's already done what had to be done. Everything's just as it was,' I replied crisply.

He got to his feet, lit a cigarette and went to look out of the window. I heard him breathing.

The cowering dog took refuge in a corner, and followed all my tired movements out of the corner of its eye.

'Everything's just as it was,' I repeated.

The smoke from his cigarette rose in circles and dissolved in the air.

'Why did you throw it away?' he asked me in a tone of voice that I had never heard him use before.

'It came out all by itself, I...'

'No, no,' he broke in. 'Why did you flush the toilet?'

I stopped and thought for a moment, because I didn't really know either.'

The dog went on staring at me, and that phrase echoed around in my head: '*Suttu 'n palazzu c'è 'n cani pazzu, te pazzu cani stu pezzu ri pani.*'

'Perhaps out of fear,' I replied.

'Fear of what?' he asked me.

I shrugged my shoulders, but he couldn't see me.

'You should have shown it to me,' he said.

'What difference would that have made…' I replied, tears beginning to sting my eyes again.

Then he turned around and said, 'I'm sorry.'

Everything's as it was.

Is everything as it was?

★ 22 ★

*Y*ou're almost black and I'm white as a q-tip, you're cheerful and I'm always melancholy.

I remember your yellow car very clearly: a yellow Fiat 127, an old model, you never see them around any more. It was funny, it looked like a cartoon, and we were the main characters. You had a mackintosh the same shade, canary yellow. For me you were 'the lady in yellow'. You had two earrings that looked like sweets, yellow and soft with a slight dip in the middle. I watched them as you drove. I looked at the mole behind your ear, the mole that identified you as my mother. You were that mole. Without that mole you wouldn't have been yourself, not even with the yellow mackintosh and not even with the sweets in your ears.

After lunch we stayed on our own and played like two sisters only a few years apart. You spoke to me and I listened to you. You spoke to me because while I was listening to you I was serious and moved my head as though to say, 'I understand, don't worry, go on.'

You told me so many things, Mamma, and none of

them are in my head now, but perhaps they've taken root
in my soul.

Afterwards, when you were tired of talking, I asked you,
'Mamma, where are we going today?'

You shrugged, giving me a trusting smile, and said,
'Who cares? Let's just get in the car and see where it takes
us!'

That yellow 127 was enchanted, it always took us to
different places, and to me those places were enchanted
too. Anonymous places, deserted, grey squares, the houses
of chattering and theatrical relations, the beauty parlour
run by your best friend, the one you exchanged important
confidences with, thoughts about marriage and husbands.
Sitting on a stool, I studied your body, covered with creams
and oils, I can still smell their perfume, I only have to think
about it.

Your words and your friend's words have remained
fundamental for me: I think it was in that room in that
beauty parlour that my sexual journey began. I think it was
there that I first heard talk about men, and first began to
form a bit of an idea about them. I was all ears, I was
always discovering something new, some new curiosity was
always being satisfied. Every day, when I asked, 'Mamma,
where are we going?' I hoped you would say, 'To the
beauty parlour!'

The 127 was our nest, our refuge. From what? Time,
perhaps. You were twenty-five or maybe even less, I was
nearly five, but we both sensed that time would steal
something very precious from us: our levity.

When you swapped the yellow 127 for a red car, our relationship changed, and I was forced to go alone to the enchanted places, the places of illusions.

'Tomorrow your daughter will be able to walk the roads of life alone, the roads woven of tears and dreams, and perhaps her wound will be in her heart.'

Do you remember those words?

I remember them. Every day.

★ 23 ★

'*I*'m going to buy some cigarettes,' he said as he left, slamming the door behind him.

I was smoking the last one, lying on the sofa, transfixed by the pictures and the voices on the television. I nodded, looking straight ahead of me.

When I heard the lift door opening and closing again, it was as though a flash of lightning had suddenly passed through me and filled me with superhuman energy. I ran to the window and grabbed his mobile phone from the sill.

Frantically fingering the keypad, I dash through the messages in his inbox and there's nothing there to give me any concern, although for a moment I have a sense of foreboding that he might have put another girl's number under my name or his mother's. Then I run through all the texts of the messages and that hint of foreboding fades away.

Suddenly a loud cough right behind me makes me start, and I feel the air stirring my hair.

I look at her and say, 'What the fuck do you want, I'm

busy. This isn't the time.'

The woman smiles at me, and whispers to me in a croak, 'I like what you're doing. You've got to know everything. Go on, go on checking his every move, follow his every footstep and listen carefully to his every word: he could be lying to you at any moment. I'm here to help you, to make you realise that reality isn't as you imagined it, it's actually very different.'

'Really?' I say contemptuously, 'and what would you know about that?'

She doesn't reply, but goes into the kitchen and pours a little water into her glass. Without saying a word, she turns towards me and inverts the glass of water. To my astonishment the water doesn't fall to the ground but instead follows a precise and perfect horizontal line. A line that stops a few inches from my nose.

I look at the woman and ask her in amazement, 'What is this?'

She folds her arms and with a smile she replies, 'This is your reality. Transparent, resolute, fluid. You poured it out where it seemed most appropriate to pour it, and now you're living in it, but the space in which you've liberated it isn't one that belongs to you. What you see before your eyes is your reality, your true reality, in the place where it should be: in a perfect straight line flowing in different directions simultaneously. That line is you.'

'So what you're trying to tell me is that I've made bad choices? Is that it?'

She shakes her head and comes over to me, sending

ripples through the water that still hangs over the room.

'What I want to tell you,' she says, 'is that until now you've concealed your true nature because you're attracted by the idea of a peaceful, normal life. But that isn't what you want, it never has been. And what you're doing now, checking up on him, is a sensational gesture on your part: the first in a long series. That's why I say to you: enough of this nonsense, take a good look at what's in that bloody mobile, and think hard about what you find.'

The rapid stream of words makes her cough again and, while the convulsions make her tremble and twist, she disappears. She fades away.

The little stream that floated a few inches from my nose vanishes as well, while the sounds and the cold of the room are heard and felt once more.

Not upset in the slightest, as though I had just opened the front door to a neighbour asking to borrow a couple of lemons, I went on running through the fascinating data supplied to me by that diabolical little machine.

A new name jumps out from among his incoming calls: Viola. So who the fuck is this Viola?

All of a sudden, sweet but forbidden features appear in my mind. Two long, well-manicured hands, two slender, agile legs supporting a perfect arse. Suddenly the woman of his dreams appears before my eyes.

A thin, pungent layer of fear insinuates itself between the folds of my muscles. My mouth contorts and begins to tremble, while my heart thumps harder and harder. The cold of the room mixes with a rare sensation of warmth that makes me sweat and shiver at the same time.

And while a series of obscene photographs fills my mind, dragging me to dark and unexplored places, he opens the door.

⋆ 24 ⋆

One is tall and thin, with a burned face and a brown shawl that completely envelops her. She shows me her wrists that have been slashed.

One is small and blonde, with blue eyes, a purple hat and a purple shawl. She looks like a circus artiste. Her legs are stumps.

A mother and a daughter stand hand in hand. The daughter has a white dog that she's holding by the collar. The little girl's name is Obelinda and she's wearing a brown floral blouse buttoned up to the neck. Her mother is almost identical, although her eyes are a different colour. They have gassed themselves.

A Turkish couple smile, they look as though they just emerged from their own wedding. They're happy and content, she's wearing a pretty pink dress. I saw them smashed against the wall by a car.

When my soul returns to my body, my head is heavy and the first thing I think is: what death do my ghosts think I have died?

⋆ 25 ⋆

As we watch a comedy film that doesn't make us laugh, Thomas tells me a dream he has had.

We are sitting at a sumptuously laid table with a brilliant white tablecloth; the courses have been arranged in an elegant and orderly fashion. Pouring some red wine into a glass, I clumsily knock it over on to the tablecloth, making a purple stain that spreads across the white cloth. Then I start crying, I say I'm sorry, I'm sorry; he kisses me and tells me it's nothing, that it could just as easily have happened to him. He demonstrates that he's equally capable of spilling his wine on the tablecloth and making a stain. But I go on crying, saying it's all my fault. His stain covers mine and he says, 'You see? No one will notice, the whole tablecloth's dirty now.'

He falls silent and looks at me without speaking.

I know he's afraid. I know he knows that I'm afraid. We both know that this bloody fear will kill us. I'm too weak to kill him because, in the end, I like fear. But I like the desire to go on loving him even more.

Today, once again, he left without saying goodbye. And
yesterday he came home without a surprise present: no ice
cream (he used to bring me an ice cream almost every
evening, with loads and loads of cherries), no film from the
video shop, not even a kiss.

Yesterday as he was brushing his teeth I came into the
bathroom without knocking, and I saw him kneeling on
the floor peering into the toilet bowl.

'What are you doing?' I asked him.

Embarrassed, he drew himself upright and replied,
'Nothing…'

I immediately understood the cause of his unease and,
at the same time, his curiosity.

'I flushed it away,' I said, 'There's nothing to see.'

'I know, I'm not crazy like you,' he replied cruelly,
slaying me with his eyes.

As in the first months of our affair, we aren't making love.
But back then, abstaining before immersing ourselves in
one another was a wonderful erotic game. Now it's a
source of unbearable pain, but I know it would be much
more unbearable if we actually did make love. It's as
though his awareness of my sexuality has shrunk and is
starting to crumble. I no longer want to fall in love with
him, to be inside him.

His body was like a musical instrument. He was a
marvellous grand piano, studded all over with white keys
and black keys, and my fingers started playing it fearlessly,

and yet they moved clumsily. I had no score, but his sighs
and the light in his eyes told me that my melody
bewitched him.

His body was a perfect contrast, his thick, burgeoning
eyebrows spread out like a patch of hair allowed to grow at
will. And his penis was a perfect fusion of angelic candour
and devastating demonic power.

'You don't love me any more.'

'Is that a question?'

'No,' I answered.

'You're the one who's stopped loving me,' he said.

'What's destroying us?' I asked him.

'We are,' he replied.

'Go if you're going,' I said.

★ 26 ★

*N*ow I know who Viola is.

Throughout all those weeks she's had him many times, and she's made love with him in every position, and I saw them having a coffee, hand in hand, during a lunch break. And her laughter constantly changed and his body transformed itself like soft clay into a body that was different every time. And he loved her on every occasion, whatever face or voice she was wearing that day.

I met her yesterday when I went into the pet shop where she works. She's young, she isn't beautiful, I don't think any of the others are really beautiful, but I do think she's his type, I'm convinced she could be. My first impulse is to hit her and kick her without losing my temper, coldly, deliberately. Strike her on that tight-fitting top, stretched over her enormous breasts.

A man called her by name from the other side of the shop, and that name was Viola.

I gritted my teeth as though I wanted to break them.

She looked at me sweetly and said, 'Are you looking for something? Can I help?'

If you really want to do something, help me to take away those horrible images that are rooting themselves in my imagination. Please put your panties back on and get off that sofa; arrange your hair and twist it into a braid, reapply your lipstick and do up the zips of your boots. Put on your scarf and your coat. And when you walk through that door don't say goodbye, just whisper, 'This is the last time we'll see each other. It was nice, you're marvellous,' as you look at him lying there, powerful and naked, and wondering why you're leaving.

And when you go through that fucking door don't cry, love. Don't cry, that would hurt me too much. The idea that those big green eyes of yours might never again see the light of the sun because I would have blinded them with the light of my fire.

Viola looks at me while with startled eyes I watch the whole scene of my film play itself out.

'You're Melissa, aren't you?' she asks.

I nod and reply clumsily, 'Yes, why?'

'I've seen you on TV a few times. I like you,' she goes on smiling. What the hell are you smiling at?

'And I've read your book,' she goes on, 'I really liked it, although I'd have written it differently myself...'

Go fuck yourself, bitch. Go on, just show me what you would have done. Take a piece of paper and a pen and write a book, if you're capable of it. But all you're capable of is straddling the dick of the man who belongs to me, who will never give himself to you as he gave himself to me.

'I don't need anything, thanks. I've got to go now,' I say as I make for the exit.

She watches me going without a word and I know perfectly, I CAN SEE THEM, I see that her eyes have become a boundless green marsh that will soon, very soon, swallow me up.

⋆ 27 ⋆

Only a few weeks had passed since that night in Cosenza we were on a train taking us to the place where we would celebrate New Year's Eve on our own.

'Do you have any idea where we could go?' I had asked him.

'A quiet place,' he had answered, 'far away from everyone.'

So we had rented a little red house surrounded by trees, lost among the Umbrian hills. It was red as a cherry, small and red.

In there, we said, our dreams met at night, wherever we ourselves might be.

'When we're far away from each other our dreams will be here, and they'll meet, we'll see them twining in the air and they will dance in a close embrace to a symphony that hasn't yet been composed,' he had said to me.

Inside, the house had yellow walls and terracotta floors, and if we walked around barefoot we could feel a vague, faint warmth spreading around the whole of our bodies.

Once inside, it was almost impossible to leave. I think a

thin, poisonous cloud hung in the air above the bed and kept us from getting up. Three days passed as though the hours, the minutes, the seconds, the day and the night belonged to other galaxies, other worlds. In that suspended red world, above the great green breast of those hills, the only thing that quivered with life was love, a gigantic, lost, stunned love; I sipped slow and long, I gulped it down, a love that allowed us to stroke one another and sometimes to kiss, but never to plunge into the deepest, blindest darkness of passion.

His body was soft and motherly, I stretched myself out on top of him and was no longer afraid.

'If we were ever to part,' I said, 'who would I tell my funny stories to? When something funny happens I can't wait to tell you about it.'

Who will I tell my funny stories to now? And do such funny things really happen?

I don't know, I don't really think so.

Perhaps what I flushed into the sewers wasn't something human, but the fruit of an extreme feeling whose name I've forgotten.

⋆ 28 ⋆

At four o'clock this morning I was woken by a voice that led me to the study. It was the woman in brown with the slashed wrists.

I looked at her, frightened, and she grinned lopsidedly.

Often, during my nightmares, I have felt an oppressive weight that kept me from screaming, from calling for help, from running. The same thing often happens to me in reality as well, and it happens when I can't keep track of myself and my ghosts.

'Pick it up,' she said to me, nodding to the pen on the desk.

I didn't move.

'I said pick it up!' Her narrow lips didn't move, but I understood.

'What do I have to do? I asked her, half frightened, half curious.

'You know what you've got to do. Don't be an idiot and pick up that bloody pen, hurry up.'

I picked it up and held it as though it was an electronic probe. I clutched it very tightly.

I went over to him. He was asleep, the sheets wrapped untidily around him without covering him up. His lips were half open, his feminine eyelashes very, very long. He looked like a beautiful little girl.

His chest was bare, so I brought the tip of the pen to the skin with the intention of tearing it. And then eating it, and not digesting it.

I brought it a little closer and my eyes filled with tears. I pressed the pen against his chest, but I didn't plunge it in. I let a drop of blood colour his white, white skin.

I remembered a line from a song: 'Maybe it's not quite legal, but you look great covered in bruises.'

I woke him up to make love. To heal his wound.

And mine.

And the deeper he plunged, the more he healed me, the more he healed me the more ashamed I grew, the more I longed for death, the more he said he was waiting for it.

And when he made love to me, pressing me close, drowning his love and his desperation inside my madness and my desperation, I heard a Sicilian voice call 'Iettiti, Vora, iettiti' – 'Blow, north wind, blow.' All my madness floated to the surface, stimulated by my echo. Not the kind of wind that cleans and refreshes, but a wind that brings with it detritus and ancient breaths, ghosts and memories.

And then I disappeared.

And then he disappeared.

★ 29 ★

I remember that in our sitting room there was a grotto, and in the grotto there was the statue of the Madonna.

I remember that she was bleeding, and that the child she held in her arms was bleeding too.

I spoke to her and you came in from the other room to ask me who I was talking to.

I didn't listen to you and went on talking in a language you didn't know.

You had a word with Father Pasqualino and he told you to try and record my voice.

You did, but when you played it back the tape was blank.

Then you talked to Dad and he hit you and then he cried, admitting that that morning he himself had seen a man walking unperturbed through the kitchen.

You went to see Father Pasqualino again and he came the following afternoon to bless the house.

As we walked him to the gate I started running and shouting that there were dozens of snakes coming after me.

Then you took me to a psychologist and he told you that I was suffering from depression and hallucinations.

I was five years old and didn't know those words.

You told me that depression was deep sadness and hallucination was deep euphoria.

When you told Dad what the doctor had said he hit you again and then he broke all the windows in the house.

I remember that in the years that followed you brought me to your friends' houses and made me walk through all the rooms, asking me which were inhabited by spirits and which were not.

I pointed to the corners of the house and then I fled.

Until the age of eight I used to see a shadow darting past and I could never make out what it was.

I went back to the psychologist and he sent me to a psychiatrist who told me to make my madness bear fruit as a way of freeing it.

I drew, but I couldn't colour anything in without going over the edges.

I bought a guitar, but I was afraid that the strings would cut my fingers.

I wrote and something inside me moved.

I wrote, I wrote, I wrote lots and lots and then I became famous.

And the thing I had freed came back and invaded me.

Killing me.

⋆ 30 ⋆

*O*nce you and I went for a walk in the country. I had a long stick to help myself climb steep slopes, and every now and again I cynically squashed any lizards that passed close by.

You were pregnant, and your belly was hard and swollen. I was worried that the lizards might hurt you, I was afraid that the whole world might hurt you. So I protected you with my little body, and followed you everywhere you went.

We stopped to sit under a big magnolia with white flowers, I remember that the sap spilled from part of the trunk, and I stuck my finger in; under the magnolia there was a tiny pond in which we bathed our feet. It was spring and the world seemed like Eden.

Countless butterflies and dragonflies swirled, suspended between heaven and earth; it was as though they wanted to keep us company, but never found the courage to come too close.

'You see those?' you said, pointing to the dragonflies. 'They can turn into women.'

'Women?' I asked you, fascinated.

'Yes, women. They come and get you at night in the form of insects and destroy your dreams, they put terrible spells on you, and they can even kill you…' you said, opening your eyes wide.

'Why?' I cried excitedly.

'They're women who pray against you, they kneel before a cross and loosen their hair and repeat magic phrases that no one knows.'

'Women on their knees… and do you know these magic phrases?' I wanted to know them too.

You shook your head and continued: 'But I know magic phrases to chase away the *ronni ri notti* – the night-women.'

'The night-women. They're the women who turn themselves into dragonflies and fly at night…' you said.

'Oh, yes.'

'The next morning you know they've come because your hair is woven into tiny, almost invisible braids that are impossible to undo.'

'Impossible?' Now I could only muster single words.

'Not impossible exactly… you have to spray your hair with oil and recite these phrases,' – you took a deep breath and your huge belly swelled until it seemed about to burst – 'Holy Monday, Holy Tuesday, Holy Wednesday, Holy Thursday, Holy Friday, Holy Saturday, Sunday the night-women will lose their wings.'

I sat there with my mouth open and whispered. 'Beautiful…'

'And remember: every time you see a dragonfly, kill it. If you let it live, it's more likely that you will die.'

We went on splashing our feet in the water while I allowed myself to fill up with the fascination of your stories.

'I hoped you would come back soon,' I say to him as I finish the last of the food from my empty, dirty plate.

'Sorry, I had problems at work,' he replies, embarrassed.

I'm embarrassed by lies and hypocrisy, they make me feel small and insignificant, they make me slide into the certainty that the other person thinks me stupid, inferior, untrustworthy. In this case, mad.

I summon up all my courage and say, 'Please tell me – who's Viola?'

'Who's Viola?'

'Who's Viola?' I reply.

'Oh yeah, she's the one who let me have the dog,' and he points to the little mongrel crouched beside us, gazing up at us, those eyes that I'm seriously starting to love.

'Oh, I get it… and it was so important that you had to store her number on your phone?' I ask harshly.

He shrugs and says, 'What's so important about that?'

I leap to my feet and react violently. 'What the hell do you mean, what does it matter? It's fucking important, that's what it is!'

He shrugs again, and this time his expression has changed. 'Ok, we've bumped into each other in the bar a couple of times, we've had a sandwich together… nothing more.'

'I bet! Nothing more? What else would you have wanted? A sandwich and that's that? In fact, I don't really see why you'd have wanted to share it with her,' I say, looking into his eyes, aware that mine are exploding from their sockets.

I stare at him and imagine him looking at her, I work my way inside him and hear his thoughts, telling him over and over to leave me. At that moment he's thinking that I'm making his life difficult, and as far as I'm concerned that's the last thing I'd like to do. But right now I just want to analyze, understand, take possession of all the security I lack. I know, I know, at any moment he's going to slam the door and he'll never come back, he'll leave me bleeding and faded on this floor; I'll gradually disappear and stop annoying him. But right now he's got to take my hands and reassure me.

As for him, he's not the kind to withdraw from a discussion. He's the kind of person who likes to reason, to make me reason, but he can't do it. He couldn't say, 'Ok, you're being a pain in the arse, so I'm out of here,' that's not his way. He stays here with me and looks at me and sometimes he smiles at me without resentment. I hate his goodness, his tolerance. He makes me feel so unworthy, so wretched and pitiful, with my tendency to hide, to seek refuge, to sink my face into the pillow, to escape my problems. I'm not capable of being so self-possessed, so empathetic.

Then he takes my hands and whispers, 'I love only you.'
And I don't believe him. Not for a moment.

Don't ask me why, don't tell me, forget it. I just don't
believe him.

Then he talks to me about freedom, he says he lacks it. He
says I'm tearing off his wings. How naïve of me, I thought
I myself was his freedom, that I was his wings, and that
with me he'd be able to go wherever he wanted, he would
have stayed perched on my back and guided me among the
clouds, among the storms, together we would have looked
down on buildings from on high, and laughed at the
stupid, impotent men struggling their way along the
streets, dragging themselves along like sacks of potatoes.

He tells me he has the right to meet whoever he feels
like, he says that that isn't why his love will shrink, he just
says, 'You've got to trust me.'

And as for me, I have the right to die, to destroy myself,
to feel my belly crumbling, to go mad and meet my ghosts,
to become their puppet.

I have the right to yield to instinct. I have the right to
cry and feel good as I do so. And I'll also have the right to
think that if he feels suffocated, clearly I'm no longer the
delicate, flowing wave that softened and dissolved him. It
means that I'm the storm now and he's alone and he can't
find shelter anywhere.

Except with Viola and her normality.

⋆ 31 ⋆

*W*hy do you beat your red-tipped wings like that, lovely dragonfly? Settled on that white wall with your black body, you look like a word on a badly-written page. Why do your wings swell each time you breathe? It's as though you were brooding hatred, rancour, rage. You've settled just a few centimetres from his photograph… ah no, dragonfly, we don't do that. I come over to you and take his photograph and put it to my chest and you look at me, disillusioned and in tears, as I dart glances back at you, likewise full of hatred, rancour and rage. Are you going mad now? Your flight is uneven now, and imprecise, I see you're running out of breath. And if I show you his photograph from a distance, what will you do, thank me?

I won't kill you, don't worry. I'd rather see you die slowly.

I know I shouldn't have slid that horrible message under the door, dragonfly, but what do you expect me to do, it's written in my blood that I must destroy everything that wants to destroy me.

Don't say anything, because you don't know anything.

You don't know what it is to be abandoned, you know nothing of the battle of love. Don't you understand that each time you immerse your big green eyes in his you're stripping me of part of my life, the air that I breathe? If you take away my breath, he won't be able to love it any more, he won't be able to smell it.

My mother, the same mother I'm talking to now, told me that dragonflies must be killed and forgotten. But I want to see you suffer a little, I want to play with your life and keep you hanging on this thin little thread, like a sadistic Fate.

I'll tell you about that time we went to the river and it was an amazing day, the rocks were sparkling and the plants showed no sign of death or decomposition. Everything was big, wonderful, strong.

I've always been used to swimming in the sea, battling with the waves, feeling that exciting fear filling me up when the blue was so dark and so deep that I couldn't see anything. I've always confronted infinite spaces, with vague horizons. I liked it, but I didn't love it. In my heart I wanted to swim in something visible, clear, with precise contours that I could see, that I could cling on to.

So when he suggested going to the river I gave a leap of joy and kissed him and whispered in his ear, 'Don't chicken out, today I want to know that we can make love in the river.' And he said, 'We'll see,' as though it was a challenge.

And our love-making really was lovely and joyous and playful, with the water splashing off our warm bodies in a thousand glittering droplets. And I felt like a mermaid with her triton, king and queen of the water, of that lonely place, that beauty.

Or I could tell you about that time when I was in a hotel, in a far-off place in South America, and I felt ill and I was shivering with cold. But my body was fine and my heartbeat was regular. And without a word he drew me to him and talked to me gently and then gradually the tears dissolved on my skin and yielded to my smile. And he said that that night I could forget who I was, what I was for the people out there. He whispered that that night I was the woman he loved and nothing more, that everything else was nothing but a silly joke.

I could tell you that I love everything about him, and I wouldn't be lying.

Can you explain to me why the hell you have two little red dots on the ends of your two wings? Did you think you would pass unnoticed, did you want to show yourself off, did you want to look seductive?

When the keys rattle behind the door she understands that the time has come to go. This, I think, is just a warning.

⋆ 32 ⋆

*I*n the corridor of our house there was a giant stain, right beside my room. I thought it was the profile of Alfred Hitchcock. Every time I walked past it at night I started running with my eyes shut, and then slipped under your covers, still shaking with fear. Or rather, first I watched you sleeping. I was standing by your side of the bed and watching you for minutes at a time, moving my head as kittens do when drunk on their own curiosity. Tears came to my eyes because you filled me with tenderness, lying there like a little girl, with your serene and heedless eyelids. Then Hitchcock came back and cast his shadow over my eyes and I fell back into darkness and desperation, in the certainty of being alone. And then I sought your warmth.

One night, as I was running with my eyes shut, I didn't notice that the door to your bedroom was closed. I ran like an untamed horse, unaware of anything, aware only of the night and its shadows. So I crashed into the door-handle, I bumped my eye with greater violence than anything I had then experienced, but I pretended everything was all right so as not to worry you. I slipped as always into your bed and went painfully to sleep. The next morning the blood was dry and dark on my cheeks. As you washed my face, concerned about what had happened to me, I looked at myself intensely in the mirror and what I saw there was a divine, saintly figure. A bleeding child, a child that quenched itself with its own mucous membrane.

⋆ 33 ⋆

'Have you any idea how idiotic you've been?' he says to me without losing his temper, but with his eyes moving from one side of my face to the other.

'What was I supposed to do? She's testing us,' I reply.

'But testing us with whom, with what?' he says, angry now.

'With you,' I snarl candidly.

'You know you're an utter maniac?' he shrieks, his voice almost as high-pitched as a woman's.

I defend what's mine.

'That poor thing came to me in tears, saying that you left a threatening message under the door of the shop! You're completely out of your mind!' he continues.

'Aha!… so… she went to see you!' I exclaim furiously. 'She came to see me too, did you know that?'

'When?' he asks, startled.

'First you tell me if you've fucked her. Or more simply: tell me if you're in love with her or what…' I say, pointing a finger at his chest.

'Fucking hell! Nothing like that, but how on earth can

I get you to believe me?' He's desperate, and he puts his arms around me. 'Why do you go on hurting yourself? Why do you think she means anything to me?'

I pull away from him and look him straight in the eyes.

'Because I can feel it,' I whisper.

After an incalculable period of time suspended between silence and complete impotence he asks, 'When did she come?'

'She left just before you got here. She flew out of the window,' and I point to it.

'What the f--' he exclaims.

'Dickhead. I didn't kill her. She came in a different form. And I recognised her. She wanted to pull a fast one on me, the whore, but she didn't succeed,' I say proudly.

He shakes his head and goes into the other room. Without a word.

Fear holds me by the hand now, and my trembling never ceases for a moment. I'm trembling now as I write, I tremble when I'm eating, I tremble as I let the water flow over my body, I tremble as I look at him, as I stare at the sky, I tremble as flocks of birds make shapes and patterns in the Roman sky. I spend hours staring at them from the window as they perform pirouettes and veer to the right and then to the left, making circles, whirlwinds, they look like hairy moles, then they plunge down, down, to the branches of the trees.

I tremble. I tremble as everything vibrates in the world,

in the air, I tremble because I know that there's still life out there and I can't live it.

I need to look at the life I have inside me, that dark life, disconnected from all the others, I need to live inside myself, because outside no one can let me live. I thought he was capable of letting me live, and wouldn't let me die one day at a time. But that's what he's doing, and I'd rather he killed me all of a sudden, once and for all, with a well aimed blow.

⋆ 34 ⋆

*L*ying on my stomach on the bed, my face suffocating in the pillow, I put my arms behind my head and slowly start to braid my hair.

'Holy Monday, Holy Tuesday, Holy Wednesday, Holy Thursday…' I murmur.

I braid slowly and diligently, taking tiny bunches of hair between my fingers.

I think that if I do this before she does, nothing will happen to me.

My body is arched, my arms hurt because of the position I have assumed, like a spider trapped in its own web.

I braid five or six bunches of hair, run my fingertip along the plait and feel it, smooth, hard and very small.

I tell myself that this way she can't hurt me.

But all of a sudden I think of him, and I think that he's exposed to danger too.

And what if the dragonfly came tonight and braided his hair? He'd be bound to her for ever, and I'd never be able to have him back, not even if I cut myself into tiny, tiny little pieces and slipped under his shoes.

So, at night, I will cuddle up next to him and when he shuts his eyes I will lightly, silently, braid his hair.

And he will be safe. We will be safe.

★ 35 ★

*T*hat time when I grew wings and my eyes dimmed till they were sightless, his absence became inevitable.

Now I have gulped her down in a single mouthful, because she was the only thing I could eat, because nothing now can give me as much nourishment as a human being. What I want is women's flesh, the flesh of a wicked, terrible woman, a dragonfly-woman.

I am something different and dark.

I am the impalpable fog and the terrible wind that shakes the branches, I am mean and murderous jealousy, I am the love I have lost and will never regain. I am a tangle of memories and joys that have begun to rot and decompose into humus for my obsessions to grow in.

I am a huge, stretched, white sheet on which the images of my love affair are projected and every memory becomes a source of unease, of obsession. My desire is not to distort reality, it's an inexplicable instinct to make my life difficult and unruly. In his face I see nothing but intolerance, lies and discomfort. I can no longer think of him, imagine him happy.

I'm a bat and I've just swallowed the dragonfly. We spent hours shut up in a bell jar, which our breath made invisible. She broke off one of my wings and I licked away the blood; my tiny, red tongue healed the wound, then my pointed teeth tore her face and I ate it. Her body was still vibrating, you should have seen it, Mamma. A body without a head, still moving, blood still flowing through its arteries. It really was a most beautiful sight, the bell jar was splashed with loads of blood and I licked it in a sign of victory.

I have destroyed my house and upturned my memories. My antennae are too weak, my eyes are completely blind. I swallow everything I find in my way, and I don't care if I swallow him too.

I have no more time to remember, to reinvent myself, to let the tapeworm move its body and make me a spectator of my past.

I have no more time.

Because now, I'm sure of it, nothing is the fruit of my imagination and my fear.

Now everything's real, palpable.

If my fantasies touch me now, I'm no longer afraid, because now I know that they're here to help me. They're here to let me live unscathed, or else to make me live in an abyss for the rest of my life.

For me, one life has the same value as another. If he isn't there, one fate weighs as much as another fate.

★ 36 ★

I hear his shoes stopping outside the door, silently observing, thinking, folding in on themselves and turning around, going on their way and leaving me on my own. And my bed has never been so big or so depressed, it has never been so deep and wickedly comforting. I can already feel his skin brushing mine, his tears mingling with mine, and it's only a sensation, yes, a sensation, because nothing of whatever happens, nothing, absolutely nothing is real. He's writing something, bent over the desk with his eyes drowning in his heart; I feel like a tiny ant, lying on that big, terrible bed. I wish I was even smaller, and transparent. I wish he could squash me once and for all. I breathlessly seek warmth from a strip of duvet, my fingertips become aware that it is crumbling away, and nothing is left. My body is just a piece of bloodless flesh, thrown into a refrigerated cell to wait for someone to buy it and cook it and eat it and do with it what he will. My body alone exists, and it is a fictitious body.

The mattress yields to support a weight and I pretend I haven't felt a thing.

Two blue eyes like yours look at me and smile at me. I whisper 'Mamma', but she shakes her head and smiles sweetly at me.

'You've got to go,' she says. 'You've got to leave and you've got to understand.'

I pretend I haven't heard anything.

'Look at me,' she cries, shaking me, 'look into my eyes.'

I look at her, and there are words inside. At first they're confused, scribbles dripping with ink, then gradually the letters assume a concrete form and fit together into phrases. It's a letter. It looks like a woman's handwriting, young, showy writing; there's an incredible vitality in the 'o's and the 'a's that inflates the letters like balloons.

The letter says:

Dear Melissa,

I'm a fan of yours. I know I'm one of many, but I hope you'll read this letter, or perhaps you'll even reply, who knows.

The story you told is not my story, it doesn't belong to me. My life is different from yours, I've had different experiences, perhaps I've made bad choices, but at least they're mine and no one else's.

And yet, dear Melissa, I feel a kind of contact with you. It's as though there were a robe pulling us tightly together. There is a connection, I've worked that out, and I hope you won't think me arrogant or anything like that. I just wanted to tell you what I think. It's something very powerful, I can't explain it.

Yours,
Penelope

PS I'm sending you a photograph, I think it's important to give a face to someone hiding behind words.

'So?' I ask the woman with eyes like yours. 'Another one who thinks she's me. So?'

'So, you fool, this might alleviate all your sufferings. Don't you understand, don't you see that the only connection between the two of you is him? The only point in common might be the love that links you to him.'

'What the hell do you mean? That it wasn't Viola but that bitch Penelope who was jeopardising my relationship with Thomas? Are you saying I'm blind, as always?'

Her eyes are sweet again, and that makes me nervous. 'No,' she says, 'she'll come after you, she doesn't exist in his thoughts. She'll come if you decide, if you go downstairs, open the letter and see the photograph she's sent you. You'll be able to decide whether to survive or to die…and quite honestly I don't know which is worse,' and she laughs, modestly putting a hand in front of her mouth.

'Shut up! Shut up… stop laughing. Tell me more clearly,' I beg.

She composes herself and says, 'Do it like this. If you want to die outright, the best thing to do is the following: you invite her over to your place one of these days, and a few hours before she turns up, you leave. You get out of there. But you really have to go for good. In the meantime, make sure that he's at home so that when she rings the bell he's the one who answers the door, and she'll be forced to accept his invitation to come in, because she's just had a long journey… and that way you'll die, but at least you'll be happy. And you'll know that everything's real, and nothing is imagined any more.'

I look at her again, I have a think, I bite my lip and whisper, 'I'll go and see her.'

I open my mailbox, see that the letter's there and I don't care, I don't give it a thought. But when I look at her photograph only one thought occurs to me: 'She's more beautiful than I am.'

And my mind's made up.

⋆ 37 ⋆

𝓘 took the train, the landscapes of Lazio and then of Umbria run parallel to my face, but my eyes are fixed on the seat opposite mine, and I am listening to a familiar but by now ephemeral voice.

He looks at me as he looked at me some months ago, straight into my pupils, with his gleaming eyes, his nostrils twitching and his mouth half open. He looks at me as he looked at me when my excess of life was still so feeble.

Now I no longer have death in my heart, because my heart has already been stripped down to nothing. Now death is advancing like a tumour; I feel it itching as it settles among my joints and muscles.

It's slow, tender, sinuous, feline. I'm not afraid. It's playing its part well, it knows how to catch human beings in its noose.

I'm abandoning him and going back to the red house on the hill, bringing his torn-up T-shirts impregnated with his smell. I don't sleep because I have a sense that if I slept I would never, ever wake up again. I huddle up on the sofa and think until the light has calmed its enthusiasms, then at night I light the fire and bring tears to my eyes by fanning the flames.

I don't know what Penelope did, I wonder if she ever came. I really hope she did, so I huddle up and think of the two of them. He says, 'Come on in, Melissa should be here any minute,' and she says, 'Oh no, I'm sorry, I'll come back later,' and then he looks at her and realises that she has beautiful eyes and a beautiful face framed by beautiful hair. But he doesn't desire her, no, not yet. She goes downstairs to wait for me, and I will never come, so she will ring the doorbell and say to him, 'Listen, she hasn't arrived yet. My train has gone… I can take the ten-thirty,' and then inevitably he will invite her up and maybe offer her a cold beer, and then, only then, will he realise, as he watches her sipping her beer, that she has the most beautiful mouth he's ever seen. And then, only then, will he decide to kiss her.

And then I go to sleep.

And when I heard you crying at night, before I abandoned you, I turned to face the other way and thought, 'Basically it's my life. I could have made it happier in the past... but I couldn't do it. Should I apologise?'

Should I apologise?

My new snake-skins are burning too quickly.

⋆ 38 ⋆

I follow him at night as he runs about the city on a moped with Penelope's breasts pressed against his back. I remember when we used to enjoy ourselves counting the holes in Rome, the huge crevasses that pierced the streets. From Trastevere to the Esquiline we counted thirty-eight holes, from Piazza Fiume to the Cassia there were too many to count.

I stagger among the stinking, narrow streets, a poodle is shitting on the steps near our apartment, the shutters are closing and the mechanics are saying goodbye to each other, arranging to meet again tomorrow, people are walking their dogs on leads. He comes out of the door, followed first by her, then by the dog. I hide behind the steps and watch the girl lifting up her dress and climbing on to the moped; she sits like Audrey Hepburn in *Roman Holiday*. Every night for three months I've gone to spy on the door of the condominium, hoping to see them come out together. I take the six o'clock train and go, and every night I wander about Rome like a junkie, except that my drug is love. And people who recognise me in the street look at me and don't talk to me, and in their eyes I see that they think I'm an addict, a star hurled too soon into the galaxy, unable to find her integrity. It's true, I haven't managed to find my integrity. I'm disturbed to the marrow.

She has a beatific smile I know very well, full cheekbones and tousled hair. He has a kind of sense of death inside, he has a dirty inheritance that he has to bear, that smells bitter.

I'd like him to fall hopelessly in love and perhaps not because his wellbeing makes me happy but perhaps because the harm I am doing myself makes me happy.

Five months later I go and stand beneath the balcony and hear her moans of pleasure, I go home and cut my skin. I carve his name with a box-cutter, I write mine, I write what I used to write in the toilets at school: 'Melissa and Thomas forever'.

He will never know of my pain, because my eyes are silent dogs that follow him, foaming at the mouth.

His happiness gives me pleasure because it's the very source of my pain, the harm I'm doing myself.

That's why I'll be eternally grateful to him. Damnation. I curse them all.

⋆ 39 ⋆

I feel the tapeworm wriggling, nestling amidst my fears and becoming their high queen.

I'm still very frightened of the dark, of monsters under the bed, the blood that might come out of the plughole. I see eyes in the walls, I feel hands beating against the floor, wolves howling from somewhere over in the hills.

At night the red house assumes a dark colour, it turns scarlet and I feel as though I'm in a huge pool of blood, floating in it along with my ghosts.

And the pain I feel confesses things to me that it has never confessed before.

Pain is the source of my life, the source of my imagination. To love I must first feel pain, to feel pain I must die.

So many things have changed, Mamma. It really is true that life is a concentration of many lives which, all added up together, can never give you a satisfactory result.

I'm just nineteen, and yet I've lived so many lives, too many. I've lived more lives than all the characters in my stories.

I've abandoned you, I've abandoned a love that pulses vividly still. I've abandoned myself.

Mamma, everything I've lived through I want to live again. I want to make the same mistakes.

I'm locked away in my room all day, the stench of cigarettes fills the air.

My dead hair scattered on the carpet, my white, tapering fingers, my yellow irises.

I think of the dragonfly Viola, and imagine myself reincarnated in her, if ever I am reborn. I reflect that while she may not have been part of my reality, mine and Thomas's, in reality she was there. She's always been there, and she's dug a deep, deep hole inside my soul, like a wizard with a sour apple.

I sleep, I look at myself in the mirror and I laugh. I laugh at myself, I laugh at my ghosts, I tell them to fuck off and they start running madly all around the house. They start chanting, they tell me I'm going to die. Today Obelinda came back to see me, and she said, 'Don't imagine you're going to get away with it.'

'I don't imagine anything of the sort,' I told her, my eyes elsewhere.

In less than a second she slipped to the foot of my bed, dilated her pupils and asked me, 'Do you know what'll happen to you afterwards, do you really know?'

'Will I keep you company in the other dimension?'

'No, worse than that,' she replied, her pupils now covering the whole of her face, cheeks, mouth, nose; none of it existed any more. Just the eyes.

'Worse, my dear,' she went on, 'don't you know what happens to those who die of love?'

I didn't move.

She touched one of my legs and I let out a shriek of pain, she burned my skin.

'What happens?' I asked with tears in my eyes.

'You'll be forced to kill the one who brought you to your death. It will be your task, it will be your purpose.'

I shook my head, I didn't want to do that.

'Yes, my darling, you will. And you'll do it because it's the only way of uniting yourself with him once more. You're his demon now, and only demons can take their own favourites with them,' she said.

'You mean you couldn't?'

'If I did I would go on being a damned soul, while he would be a free one. If you do it, drag him with you, because he must obey only you.'

'I don't want him. I'll disappear for ever and watch him love: that will be the damnation I've deserved,' I replied.

She came over to me and breathed in my face. Her breath froze my muscles.

'You stupid, spoilt little girl. You've asked for it. The other ghosts and I will hurt you so badly that you'll beg us to die a terrible death. We'll finish you off.'

When I was little I drew a closed semi-circle on a sheet of paper. I drew a little ball on each end of the semicircle and then I wrote 'love' on one side and 'hate' on the other.

⋆ 40 ⋆

Cold floor. Doors barred and shutters lowered. Lights out. My naked body, lying here. Wind on the hills. Rain. Sun. Then rain again. One week. Two weeks. Three weeks. Three days. No remorse, no kindness, no emotion. The absence of the ghosts. The sense of having attained perfection and omnipotence. Omnipotence. Omnipotence.

Then the darkness comes and grips me by the arm.

★ 41 ★

*W*hat did you do today? When someone phoned you at six in the morning and told you they'd found your daughter lying on the floor, close to death, what did you think? Did you scream, did you curse, did you feel overwhelmed with resignation? Did you think you had a mad daughter? Or did you think you had a daughter who was passionately in love? Or perhaps both?

When you took the first flight for Rome and then travelled more than a hundred kilometres to find me and when you reached the red house on the hill and didn't find anyone, just my hair scattered on the carpet, what did you call your pain?

And what was the consistency of your love when you looked at me through the glass in the door, while my wrists, slashed and now healed, were outstretched and hanging, held up by two strips of white fabric?

And what fear did you feel when you saw my eyes? When you noticed that one of them was going blind, full of clotted blood?

And would you have allowed yourself to be stroked by

my hands with their shattered nails?

And that part of me I gave you, where did it end up?

If it's still inside you, free it, let it fly. Perhaps one day it will come back to me, and we will have a great orgy of love.

hanks.

For many reasons, all different and unpronounceable, I thank: my dog Burrito, who arrived late but not too late. Simone Caltabellota who, on the other hand, arrived early. Nikki Sudden, Nic Kelman and Rocco Fortunato. Martina Donati and Melisso, plus the unborn child (who will have been born by now!) Nilo. Julieta and Bengt, Ignacio and Mario Brega.

I'd also like to thank the co-protagonist of this story even if, in my view, I've already devoted too much time to him (both in life and in the book).

And then I thank all the people who hate me, because it's thanks to them that I love myself all the more.